Squirlish

Shark in the Park

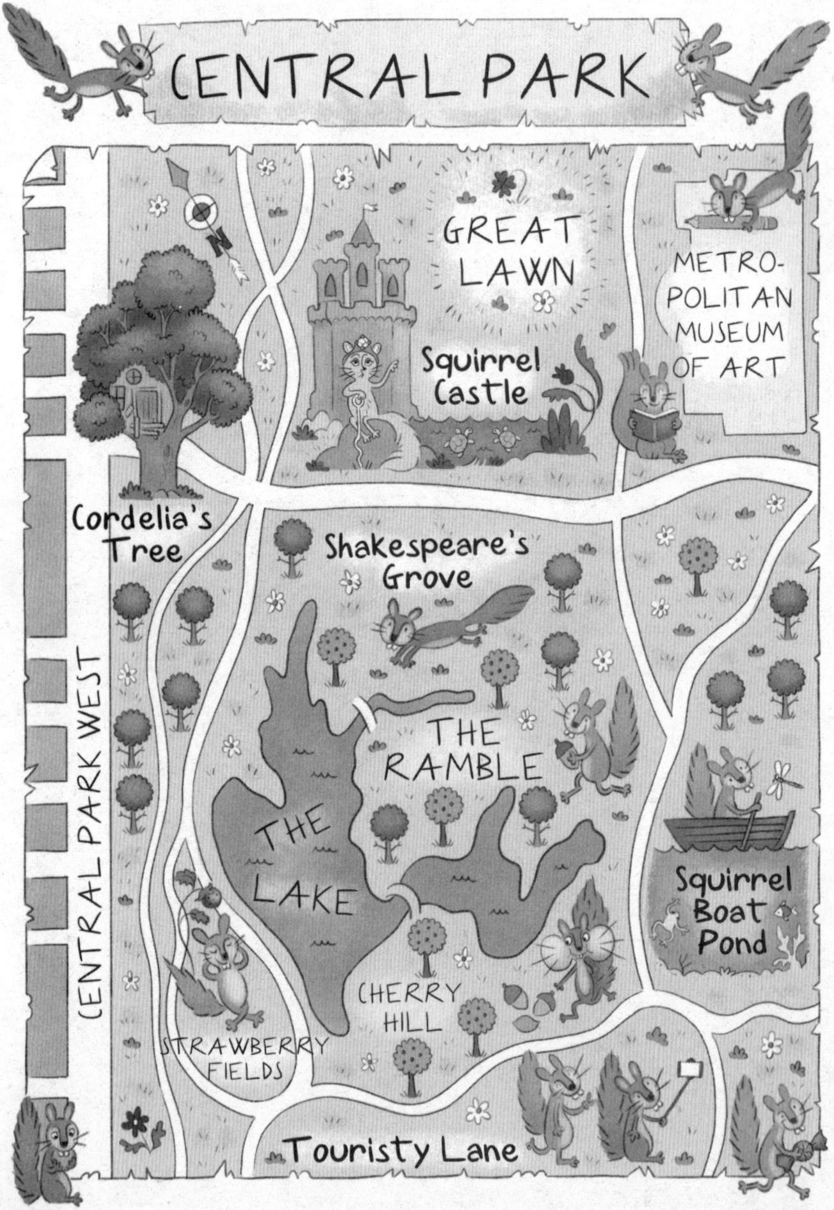

CENTRAL PARK

GREAT LAWN

METRO-POLITAN MUSEUM OF ART

Squirrel Castle

Cordelia's Tree

CENTRAL PARK WEST

Shakespeare's Grove

THE RAMBLE

THE LAKE

Squirrel Boat Pond

CHERRY HILL

STRAWBERRY FIELDS

Touristy Lane

ELLEN POTTER

Squirlish
SHARK IN THE PARK

ART BY
SARA CRISTOFORI

Margaret K. McElderry Books
New York   London   Toronto   Sydney   New Delhi

MARGARET K. McELDERRY BOOKS

An imprint of Simon & Schuster Children's Publishing Division
1230 Avenue of the Americas, New York, New York 10020

This book is a work of fiction. Any references to historical events, real people, or real places are used fictitiously. Other names, characters, places, and events are products of the author's imagination, and any resemblance to actual events or places or persons, living or dead, is entirely coincidental.

Text © 2024 by Ellen Potter
Illustration © 2024 by Sara Cristofori
Jacket design by Rebecca Syracuse

MARGARET K. McELDERRY BOOKS is a trademark of Simon & Schuster, LLC.
Simon & Schuster: Celebrating 100 Years of Publishing in 2024
For information about special discounts for bulk purchases, please contact Simon & Schuster Special Sales at 1-866-506-1949 or business@simonandschuster.com.
The Simon & Schuster Speakers Bureau can bring authors to your live event. For more information or to book an event, contact the Simon & Schuster Speakers Bureau at 1-866-248-3049 or visit our website at www.simonspeakers.com.
Also available in a Margaret K. McElderry Books paperback edition
Interior design by Rebecca Syracuse
The text for this book was set in Bookman Old Style Pro.
The illustrations for this book were rendered digitally.
Manufactured in the United States of America
0524 FFG
First Edition
2 4 6 8 10 9 7 5 3 1
Library of Congress Cataloging-in-Publication Data
Names: Potter, Ellen, 1963- author. | Cristofori, Sara, illustrator.
Title: Shark in the park / Ellen Potter ; art by Sara Cristofori.
Description: First edition. | New York : Margaret K. McElderry Books, 2024. | Series: Squirlish ; 2 | Audience: Ages 6 to 9. | Audience: Grades 2-3. | Summary: Cordelia, a human girl living with squirrels in Central Park, must protect squirrel Prince Oliver during his quest for the Royal Scepter, but Prince Oliver has other plans and is more interested in finding a shark than a scepter.
Identifiers: LCCN 2023010778 (print) | LCCN 2023010779 (ebook) | ISBN 9781665926782 (hardcover) | ISBN 9781665926775 (paperback) | ISBN 9781665926799 (ebook)
Subjects: CYAC: Squirrels—Fiction. | Quests (Expeditions)—Fiction. | Sharks—Fiction.
Classification: LCC PZ7.P8518 Sh 2024 (print) | LCC PZ7.P8518 (ebook) | DDC [Fic]—dc23
LC record available at https://lccn.loc.gov/2023010778
LC ebook record available at https://lccn.loc.gov/2023010779

For Linda
—E. P.
To Ravenswood Primary School
—S. C.

Shark in the Park

I

George the Lobster Hat

Plink, plunk! Plink, plink, plunk!

Cordelia woke up that morning to the sound of acorns hitting her tree house. The tree house was perched high up in an elm tree in the middle of Central Park. She lived there with a squirrel named Shakespeare. He had found her under a shrub when she was a baby, and he had raised her as his own.

Cordelia squinted her eyes open—
first one, then the other. She sat up and
peeked out of the little tree house window. On the grassy lawn below, she saw
her friend Isaac. He smiled and waved up
at her.

"Want to play Gorilla Kickball?" Isaac
called up.

"Be right down!" Cordelia called back.

She scrambled out of the tree house,
leapt down to a lower limb, and skipped
along the branch as nimbly as . . .
well, as nimbly as a squirrel, until she
reached a large hole in the trunk. That
was where she kept all her stuff. Some
of it were things that Viola Berry, the
park's groundskeeper, had bought for

her, like boots and a puffer jacket and a knit hat and lots of books about animals. Some other things she had found in the playground. People were always leaving interesting things in playgrounds, like plastic-bead bracelets and half-used bottles of soap bubbles and a little man made of LEGO bricks. Cordelia chose her clothes for the day and her favorite bead bracelet, and after she got dressed, she went to peek at Shakespeare. He was curled up in his nest in the tree, his bushy tail covering his eyes.

"Are you sleeping?" she whispered.

Shakespeare let out a big snore.

"That's a fake snore," she said, lifting his tail off his eyes.

"It was a real snore a second ago before you woke me up," he replied.

"I'm going to play Gorilla Kickball with Isaac."

"Are the gorillas the quiet kind of gorillas?" Shakespeare asked.

Cordelia laughed. "There are no goril-las, Shakespeare."

She gently placed his tail over his eyes again.

She climbed down to the last branch and made a springy leap to the ground, landing squarely on her feet.

"I call Gorilla!" she said.

Gorilla Kickball was a game she and Isaac had made up. It involved a lot of running and tumbling and hiding and a soccer ball.

They were having a great time, racing around and rolling in the grass, when suddenly Cordelia felt an acorn plop on her head. She looked up to see Kate, a small red squirrel, glaring down at her from a tree branch.

Uh-oh.

"I'll never understand how you can run around on those ridiculous legs of yours, Cordelia," Kate said. "They look like Popsicle sticks."

Cordelia ignored her.

"You might *act* like a squirrel, Cordelia," Kate continued. "And you might live in a tree like a squirrel, but super guess what . . . ? You're not a squirrel!"

"I'm *squirlish*," Cordelia shot back.

Shakespeare always told her that she was a little bit squirrel and a little bit girl. That made her squirlish.

"People *visit* Central Park, they don't *live* in Central Park. You don't belong here, Popsicle Stick Legs." Kate flicked her tail at Cordelia.

Cordelia's stomach started to feel *blurggy*, which is when you feel like you've eaten something that doesn't agree with you, only you haven't. Cordelia ran to her elm tree and climbed back up to the hole in the trunk. She reached into the hole and pulled out a hat shaped like a lobster. It was bright red with dangly lobster claws that hung down by her ears.

"Good morning, George," Cordelia said to the hat, and she put it on her head. Then she told the hat what Kate had just said to her.

"What are you doing?" Isaac called up to Cordelia.

"Talking to George." She pointed up at her lobster hat.

"Why are you talking to a hat?" Isaac asked.

"Shakespeare said that whenever I feel worried, I should tell the worry to George and let him worry about it instead."

"Oh." Isaac nodded. "Does it work?"

Cordelia thought about it. Her stomach didn't feel so *blurggy* anymore. Just a little *blurggy*.

"It mostly works," she said. "I think George always leaves a tiny bit of the worry for me."

She climbed back down to the ground just as Fenton the rat came running up to them.

"How do I look?" Fenton asked. He spit on his paws and groomed his whiskers.

"What did he say?" Isaac asked Cordelia.

Fenton was speaking in Chittering, which is the language squirrels speak. Even though Fenton was a rat, he hung around squirrels so much that he spoke it fluently.

"He wants to know how he looks," Cordelia translated.

"Oh! I'll tell him!" Isaac knelt down in front of Fenton. Cordelia was teaching Isaac how to speak in Chittering, and he took every opportunity to practice.

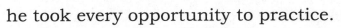

"You look very handsome," Isaac said to Fenton in Chittering.

Except Isaac's Chittering was not very good. What Isaac actually said was "You look like a furry onion dumpster."

Fenton made an unhappy squeak. "I do?"

"He didn't mean that," Cordelia said. "But why do you care what you look like all of a sudden?"

"Because of them." He pointed.

Trotting on the footpath were four large white rats. Sitting on the back of each rat, riding them like ponies, were very noble-looking squirrels. They were the queen's Royal Messengers, and it looked like they were heading straight toward Cordelia.

2
The Queen's Message

Each Royal Messenger was wearing a blue sash around their chest. If you looked closely, you could see that the sashes were actually paper wrappers from hot dog packages. Still, the Royal Messengers looked very impressive as they sat on their rats, with their well-groomed tails held high in the air.

"Those types of rats are called fancy rats," said Isaac. "We have two rats like that in our classroom. Their names are Boris and Doris. Boris can jump rope."

"They *are* very fancy," Fenton muttered. He understood English pretty well, even if he couldn't speak it.

Cordelia looked at Fenton. He seemed to droop miserably as he watched the fancy rats approaching. She took off her bead bracelet and snapped the string that held it together.

"Stay still," she said to Fenton. She strung the beads on his tail and tied the string at the top so that the beads wouldn't fall off.

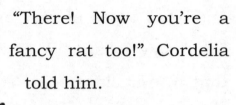

"There! Now you're a fancy rat too!" Cordelia told him.

That cheered Fenton right up.

The Royal Messengers stopped their rats right in front of Cordelia, Isaac, and Fenton. One of the Royal Messengers hopped off his rat and walked up to them.

Isaac bowed down. "I'm happy to meet you," he said in Chittering. Except what he actually said was "I'm going to squeeze you."

The Royal Messenger backed away, looking alarmed.

"He's not really going to squeeze you," Cordelia reassured the messenger.

The Royal Messenger sniffed. In his hands was a rolled-up piece of paper. He cleared his throat and unrolled the paper. It was just a napkin with a mustard stain on it, but it looked very official.

The messenger read out loud from the napkin: "Queen Isabel requests that Miss Cordelia come to Belvedere Castle immediately."

"*Me?* Why?"

The Royal Messenger looked down at the napkin, then looked up again. "It doesn't say."

"Maybe the queen wants to make you a knight," Fenton suggested.

But Cordelia was wondering if the queen had another reason for wanting her to come to the castle. Maybe the queen was going to tell Cordelia that human girls were not allowed to live in elm trees in Central Park. Not even human girls who were squirlish.

3
A Fizzmizzle

Belvedere Castle stood on a cliff above Turtle Pond. It was a fine-looking castle with all the castle-y things, like turrets and stone walls and those windows that are shaped like Christmas trees.

Once inside, it was clear to Cordelia that the castle was in a *fizzmizzle*, which was Shakespeare's word for when everyone is running around in a panic.

The Royal Cleaners were scrubbing the floors. The Royal Cooks were frantically shelling walnuts with their teeth. Even Queen Isabel was scurrying around the castle and barking orders at everyone. The only squirrel who wasn't in a frenzy was a young squirrel with a crown on his head, who was kicking a ball of tinfoil around the floor as though he were playing soccer.

"Your Highness, I have brought Cordelia to you." The Royal Messenger turned to Cordelia and said, "Curtsy to the queen."

Cordelia wasn't sure what a curtsy was, but it sounded like "courtesy," so

Cordelia turned to the queen and said, "Please and thank you."

"You're welcome," said the queen. "I've asked you here because today is Prince Oliver's birthday."

Cordelia looked at the young squirrel who was kicking the tinfoil.

"Happy birthday!" she said to him

"I'm not Oliver, I'm Cedric," the squirrel said as he gave the tinfoil ball a kick so hard, it flew up in the air. He bounced it off his head. "Oliver's upstairs being a weirdo."

"Cedric!" the queen warned her son. She turned back to Cordelia. "And because it's Prince Oliver's birthday, he will be going on a quest for the Royal Scepter."

"Which he'll never find," Cedric mumbled. "Because no one ever finds it."

"What's a Royal Scepter?" Cordelia asked.

The queen pointed to a sculpture in the corner of the room. The sculpture was made out of wood that had been gnawed into the shape of a squirrel with a large crown on his head. The squirrel was holding a stick with a fuzzy top. It looked like a tiny broom, no bigger than a finger. "That's my father, King Alonso," the queen said. "And that"—she pointed to the little broom-shaped stick—"is the Royal Scepter. It was found in the park over a hundred years ago, and it had been our kingdom's most prized possession. Then one day, five years ago, it mysteriously went missing. We've been searching for it ever since."

Cordelia didn't think the Royal Scepter
looked too amazing. But still, she had a
stuffed penguin that had fluff coming out
of its beak, and if that old penguin ever

got lost, she would search all over for it, too.

"As you know, there are many dangers for a squirrel in the park," the queen continued. "Bicycles and skateboarders. Hawks. That awful pirate, Crazy-Eye Winston. Not to mention the dogs! Since you are a . . . you know . . ." The queen paused, as though she might be saying a bad word. "Since you are a *human*, we felt we could count on you to keep Prince Oliver safe. Cedric"—the queen turned to her son—"would you please go get your brother?"

"OLIVER!" Prince Cedric shouted at the top of his lungs.

The next moment, a very young squirrel wearing a wooden sword in a belt bounded into the room. He was small and gray, and he had crumbs stuck to his tail. There was a golden crown on his head, but it had slipped sideways, so that it covered one of his eyes.

The queen introduced them as she adjusted the crown on his head. "Prince Oliver, this is Cordelia."

"Guess how many bones a shark has," Prince Oliver said to Cordelia.

"None," Cordelia answered. "Sharks have cartilage, not bones."

The prince's eyes grew wide. "*Bing, bing, bing!* You are correct, sir!"

He jumped straight up in the air, which is what squirrels do when they are especially happy. His crown toppled off his head and rolled across the room, and his sword flew out of his belt and hit the queen on the foot.

"Ouch," the queen said very quietly.

The queen put the crown back on the prince's head and gave him a quick nibble on his ear, which is the squirrel version of a kiss. "Good luck, darling."

"Better wish Cordelia luck," Prince Cedric said. "She's the one who's going to need it."

4
Twisty-Turny Slide

"Where do you want to look first?" Cordelia asked the prince once they'd left the castle.

"Underwater," Prince Oliver replied.

"Oh! You think the Royal Scepter will be underwater?"

"No, I think the shark will be underwater," Prince Oliver said.

"What shark?"

"The one Vivian told me about. She's a pigeon. She likes to sit on my windowsill. She says there's a shark in Central Park."

"I don't think there are any sharks in Central Park."

"Not even a hammerhead?"

"No."

"What about a tiger shark? Or a lemon shark? What about a basking shark?"

"I'm pretty sure there are zero sharks in Central Park."

"Oh." The prince was clearly disappointed. He thought for a moment. "Can we see the roller coaster?"

"Did Vivian tell you there were roller coasters in Central Park?"

Prince Oliver nodded.

Cordelia was beginning to think that Vivian was not the most truthful pigeon.

"Why don't we look for the Royal Scepter in the playground?" Cordelia suggested. "People are always losing things in the playground."

As they walked along, the prince kept zipping off to climb on lampposts and benches and rocks. He zigged and zagged all over the park. Cordelia zigged and zagged after him, picking up his crown each time it fell off his head. Every so often he'd give her some treasure he'd found, like an empty soda can and a candy wrapper and a blue jay feather. She kept the feather.

Once in a while, he'd stop to quiz her about sharks.

"Question. What's the most number of teeth a shark can grow in a lifetime?"

Cordelia had to guess on this one. "Three hundred."

"*Bzzz!* Incorrect. The answer is thirty thousand!"

And then he darted off again.

When they reached the playground, Prince Oliver actually stood still for a moment. He looked at all the swings and slides and climbing ropes.

"Whoa!"

"Is this the first time you've ever seen a playground?" Cordelia asked, surprised.

"This is the first time I've ever left the castle." He jumped in the air with such delight that his crown flew off his head and rolled across the grass. Cordelia ran to fetch it, but when she came back, the prince was nowhere in sight. She went into the playground

and looked around. There were loads of kids shooting down the slides and climbing on the ropes and running across the wooden bridges. But there wasn't a single squirrel in sight.

Oh no! I've lost him already!

Suddenly she heard a big commotion. It was coming from the sandbox. She ran over there to find a circle of children standing around the sandbox and staring down at it.

"What's in the sandbox?" Cordelia asked.

"Shark," one little girl said, pointing. There was a tiny little shark fin poking out of the sand. It moved this way and that, swimming from one side of the sandbox to the other. Cordelia squinted at the fin. It looked suspiciously like the tip of a wooden sword.

Plunging her hand into the sandbox, Cordelia felt around until she pulled up Prince Oliver.

The kids all *oohed*. A squirrel in a sandbox was almost as amazing as a shark in a sandbox.

"Did they think I was a shark?" Prince Oliver asked as he swiped sand out of his eyes with his paws.

"Yes."

That seemed to delight the prince. He put his paws over his mouth and made happy little squeaks of laughter.

It *was* kind of funny, but Cordelia forced her face to look serious. "You can't run away like that, Prince Oliver."

The prince stopped laughing.

"Are you mad?" he asked.

She was a little mad. But then she thought about what it must be like to live in a big old castle without

ever seeing playgrounds or lampposts or rocks.

"Do you want to go on the twisty-turny slide?" she asked him. "After that we can look for the Royal Scepter."

"Yes, please."

Cordelia put him on her shoulder, where he sat very nicely while she climbed up the ladder to the twisty-turny slide. It was one of those slides that goes round and round like a macaroni. It was very slippery, too. Isaac said that maybe they poured olive oil on it at night to make it so slippery. Cordelia had tried out all the slides in the park and this one was her favorite.

Each time they shot down the slide,

Cordelia would call out, "Look out below, buffalo!"

Each time they reached the bottom, Prince Oliver cried out, "Let's go again!"

The only problem was that it was everyone else's favorite slide too. The line to go on the slide grew longer and longer. As they waited for their turn, Prince Oliver squirmed on Cordelia's shoulder with impatience.

"Can't you tell them I'm a prince?" Prince Oliver said. "Then we won't have to wait."

"Everyone has to wait for their turn," Cordelia replied firmly. "Playground rules."

Prince Oliver grew squirmier and

squirmier. Finally, he couldn't stand it any longer. He leapt off Cordelia's shoulder and onto the shoulder of the boy in front of them, and then onto the shoulder of the girl in front of that boy, until he reached the slide.

"Prince Oliver!" Cordelia yelled up to him. "That's cheating!"

But Prince Oliver hopped on the slide anyway and down he went.

When you don't have any pants on, and your backside is made of fur, slides are especially slippery. Prince Oliver shot down that twisty-turny slide, skidding from one side to the other. He flipped upside down, and his crown fell off his head. Then, on the last twisty turn, the prince flew off the slide altogether and landed in a lady's diaper bag.

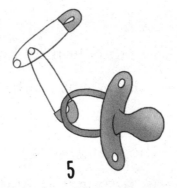

5

Diaper Lady

The lady had been sitting on a bench, reading a book while her baby was napping in its stroller. She never even noticed that a squirrel had tumbled into her diaper bag.

"Excuse me, excuse me," Cordelia said as she tried to squeeze past the boy ahead of her.

"No cutting," he said.

There were kids behind her on the ladder too, so there was nothing she could do except wait her turn. When she finally flew down the twisty-turny slide, she was too nervous to enjoy it and didn't even shout, "Look out below, buffalo!"

She scooped up the little crown from the ground. Then she hurried over to the diaper-bag lady, who was now walking out of the park, pushing the stroller with one hand and holding the diaper bag with the other.

"Excuse me!" Cordelia ran up to her, pointing to the diaper bag. "I need to get something out of that bag."

The lady looked Cordelia up and down. "You're a little old for diapers."

"It's not a diaper. It's a squirrel."

"Why would I put a squirrel in my diaper bag?"

"You didn't put him in there," Cordelia said. "He *fell* in."

"A squirrel fell out of the sky and into my diaper bag?"

Cordelia was starting to get the feeling that the lady didn't believe her.

"No, he fell into the diaper bag when he was going down the slide."

"I see." The lady stared at Cordelia for a moment. She stared at the lobster hat on Cordelia's head. Then she zipped up her diaper bag with a loud *ZZZZZP!* and hurried away.

Cordelia followed the diaper lady, but the diaper lady must have had eyes in the back of her head because she turned around and gave Cordelia the death glare.

So Cordelia had to think of a plan B.

Cordelia might not have been an actual squirrel, but she *was* squirlish. She scrambled up a fat maple tree until she got to the top. Then she leapt onto the next tree and the next tree. You've seen squirrels do that a hundred times, I'll bet, and Cordelia could spring across branches as well as any squirrel in the park. The whole time, she kept her eyes on the diaper lady below her. Occasionally, the diaper lady would look up when she heard a rustling. That was when Cordelia would freeze in place, and after a moment the diaper lady would continue walking.

Every so often, Cordelia would surprise a squirrel in one of the trees. Some of them recognized her.

"Oh, my goodness, you're Cordelia!" one of them cried out. "You're the Squirrel Girl of Central Park! Will you give my babies a nibble? Please, please, please! They're just in the nest over here. When they're older, I can tell them that the famous Cordelia once gave them a nibble."

"Okay, a quick nibble," Cordelia said. She climbed over to the nest, while she kept an eye on the diaper lady.

In a tidy nest were three baby squirrels, all smooshed together in a cuddle.

Cordelia gave each one the gentlest little nibble on the tips of their ears.

Down below, the diaper lady's baby began to cry. The diaper lady stopped walking, picked up her baby and smelled its bottom. She wrinkled her nose. Then

she sat down on a bench and unzipped
the diaper bag. Prince Oliver sprang out
and the diaper lady screamed. In a flash,
Cordelia hopped onto a sturdy branch,

swung on it three times, and then launched herself into the air. She landed in front of the diaper lady, who screamed a second time. Cordelia scooped up Prince Oliver and showed him to the diaper lady.

"See! I told you so!" Cordelia said.

It's not the best policy to tell people "I told you so," but sometimes you just can't help yourself.

"What was in that lady's bag?" Prince Oliver asked as Cordelia walked off with the prince perched on her shoulder.

"They're called diapers."

"Diapers!" he said dreamily. "I love diapers . . . so puffy and soft! I wish I had a nest made of diapers. Vivian never told me about them. She did tell me that clouds were made of water balloons, and when birds crash into them the balloons break, and that's why it rains."

"I think you might need to find some new friends, Prince Oliver."

6
The Bone Rattler

Cordelia was thinking about where they should look for the Royal Scepter next. Playgrounds seemed too risky.

"Ooh, look at that!" Prince Oliver said. He was looking ahead at a plaza that was filled with kids playing chess. There were rows and rows of long tables. Next to each player was a little wooden clock that the players slapped when they made a move.

"It's a chess tournament," said Cordelia.

The kids at the tables were very quiet and focused. Everyone standing around and watching the kids playing chess was very quiet and focused. The only things moving were the rowboats gliding on the lake behind them.

Prince Oliver began to squirm.

"True or false," Prince Oliver said, his voice shrill with excitement. "Sharks always live in the ocean."

"Um, true," said Cordelia.

"*BZZZZZ!* Incorrect! Sometimes sharks live in the LAKE!"

And then she realized! He wasn't excited about the chess tournament. He was excited about the lake *behind* the chess tournament.

Before she could stop him, Prince Oliver leapt off Cordelia's shoulder. He jumped onto one of the chess tables and dashed across it, running zigzags like squirrels do. Chess pieces flew in the air and tumbled off the board. The kids at the table screamed and threw up their hands in frustration.

Cordelia raced after Prince Oliver, but squirrels are faster than people. By the time she reached him, Prince Oliver was already standing by the edge of the lake, chatting to a squirrel who was sailing in a very tiny ship. The ship was painted green with red trim, and it had three tall masts, each one with a flag on top.

THE BONE RATTLER

Each flag was black with a white skull and crossbones on it. On the side of the ship were the words *The Bone Rattler*.

The Bone Rattler! Cordelia had heard about that ship. It belonged to the pirate Crazy-Eye Winston!

"Blimey, there are oodles of sharks in these waters," the pirate was saying to Prince Oliver. "I see a dozen of them every day. Sometimes more! If you come aboard my ship, I'll take you to them." The whole time Crazy-Eye Winston was looking at the crown on Prince Oliver's head.

"What sort of sharks have you seen?"

"Oh, let me think." Crazy-Eye Winston

gazed up at the sky, and he scratched his chin. "I've seen Yellow-Tooth Crunchers and I've seen Sharktopuses—"

"Those are made-up sharks!" Cordelia said. "Don't listen to him! He's a pirate."

"You've probably never heard of those sharks because they're so rare," the pirate said. "You only find them in Central Park. Come aboard, lad!" He patted the side of his boat. "I'll show you more sharks than you've ever dreamed of."

This was too much for Prince Oliver. He leapt straight into the water. Squirrels are not great swimmers, but they *can* swim. Cordelia, however, could not. She watched helplessly as Prince Oliver paddled his way over to the pirate while Cordelia yelled, "Come back here this minute!"

The pirate helped Prince Oliver onto the ship, and with a saucy wave at Cordelia, he sailed his ship out into the lake.

"Hey ho, the winds may blow, but this ship will never tip! Fill my nest with a treasure chest and hoopa, away we go!"

7
Blurggy

Cordelia walked alongside the lake's shore, her heart thumping. She kept her eyes fixed on *The Bone Rattler* as the ship sailed out to the middle of the lake. The ship was very small, but it was fast. The wind was taking it farther and farther away. The lake narrowed and twisted, and suddenly *The Bone Rattler* disappeared around a bend.

"Oh no!" Cordelia started running, dodging bikers and skateboarders. She crashed through a group of bird-watchers and jumped over a rottweiler. Finally, she came to a cove where she spotted the little pirate ship, bobbing in the water. Crazy-Eye Winston was standing on the deck, but Prince Oliver was nowhere in sight.

"What did you do with the prince?" Cordelia demanded, breathing hard from her run.

"The little scallywag kept *bzzzz*-ing me!" the pirate complained.

"He kept what-ing you?"

"He kept asking me questions about sharks. 'What came first, sharks or dinosaurs?' 'Can sharks see color?' 'How big is a whale shark?' And when I got the answer wrong, he'd scream '*Bzzzz!*'" Crazy-Eye Winston chattered his teeth and stomped his foot. "It was very irritating."

"You didn't make him walk the plank, did you?"

"Aye, I would have! I meant to! But when we came around the bend here, he suddenly got all excited. Then he dove straight into the water and swam to shore."

Cordelia squinted at the pirate. "You're not lying to me, are you?"

"Lass, does this look like a lying face?" He tried to make his face look innocent, but then he flicked his tail and said, "Ah, never mind. I know I have a lying face, but I'm not lying now." Crazy-Eye Winston tossed something to Cordelia. It was the prince's crown. "He dropped it when he jumped off the ship."

"Thank you," Cordelia said. "I'm going to tell the queen that you aren't so bad after all."

"Blimey, don't do that, lass!" Crazy-Eye Winston called back to her as he sailed his ship away from the shore. "I have my reputation to think about!"

Central Park was very big, and Prince Oliver was very small. Cordelia began to feel that *blurggy* feeling in her stomach. What if she couldn't find him? What if he got chased by a dog and didn't know where he was? What if he got eaten by an owl or smooshed by a skateboard? Cordelia felt all hot and sweaty. It seemed like her brain was trying to tell her something, but her heart was thumping so loudly that she couldn't hear it.

Then she remembered that George the

lobster hat was sitting on her head.

"George," she said to him, "I've lost the prince and he might be in danger, and I don't know what to do."

As soon as she told George all about it, the *blurggy* feeling in her stomach felt better. Her heart stopped thumping so loudly. Now that George was doing her worrying for her, she could do her thinking.

Why did Prince Oliver jump off the ship all of a sudden? she wondered. *What did he see?*

She looked all around her. All she could see were trees and benches and people and dogs.

Look harder, her brain told her.

She looked under the benches. She looked behind the trees.

Then she looked up. And that was when she saw it. She made a little gasping noise. Then she smiled.

"I think I know where he is, George!"

8

Wonders of the Ocean

Right across the street from the park was a large building with big white columns in front of it, the American Museum of Natural History. If you looked up over the park's wall, you could see a big banner hanging above the main entrance. The banner had a shark on it with its mouth wide open, showing its sharp triangular teeth. Around the shark were the words WONDERS OF THE OCEAN: SHARK EXHIBIT.

Cordelia went into the museum. The lobby was full of dinosaur skeletons. She knew the name of each one. Shakespeare had taught her all about dinosaurs.

She went up to the ticket window. The sign said, PAY WHAT YOU WISH.

Cordelia checked her front pockets. She had a hair tie in one of them and a crumpled foil gum wrapper in the other. Then she stuck her hand in her back pocket and pulled out the blue jay feather that Prince Oliver had given to her. She put it on the counter.

"I wish to pay with this," Cordelia said.

"Hmm." The ticket lady picked up the
feather and examined it. "Blue jay?"
Cordelia nodded.

"My favorite kind of bird." The lady smiled. "Good enough for me." The lady handed Cordelia a ticket and a map.

The shark exhibit was on the second floor. The exhibit room was dark, and there were movie screens on all the walls showing sharks swimming slowly while ocean sounds played on speakers. There were glass cases full of shark fossils and shark skeletons. In the center of the room was a life-sized model of a great white shark. The shark was huge! It was as long as four park benches put together. Beneath its pointy nose, its mouth was wide open as if it were just about to take a chomp out of something.

From inside its mouth, Cordelia heard a tapping noise. Then she heard a small voice counting: "Seventeen, eighteen, nineteen—"

Kneeling down, Cordelia looked inside the shark's mouth.

"Oh, hello, Cordelia!" Prince Oliver said when he saw her. He was counting the shark's teeth with the tip of his sword. "True or false. Great white sharks were around before dinosaurs."

"True," Cordelia said.

"That pirate didn't know the answer." Then he looked at her with a serious face. "I think Vivian was wrong. I don't think there are any real sharks in Central Park."

"No," Cordelia agreed.

"And we didn't find the Royal Scepter."

"No. But we did find a pirate," Cordelia reminded him. "And a twisty-turny slide."

"And diapers. Don't forget diapers!"

With Prince Oliver on her shoulder, they made their way through the museum and passed an exhibit all about Central Park. There was a group of people crowded around a glass case.

"A long time ago, there used to be a village right where Central Park is today," the tour guide was saying. "It was called Seneca Village, and it was started by African Americans. They had farms and churches. Children went to school in the village. But when the city wanted to build Central Park, the people who lived in the village were told that they didn't belong there. They were forced to leave. Years later, we found things in Central Park that the people of Seneca Village left behind."

Cordelia peeked into the glass case. It was full of all sorts of things—bits of broken pottery, the sole of a small shoe, a teapot. Way in the back was a strange-looking item. It looked like a tiny little broom, no bigger than a finger.

"Prince Oliver!" Cordelia said in an excited whisper as she pointed at it. "Isn't that . . . ?"

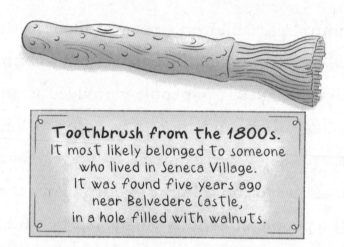

Toothbrush from the 1800s.
It most likely belonged to someone
who lived in Seneca Village.
It was found five years ago
near Belvedere Castle,
in a hole filled with walnuts.

"It's the Royal Scepter!" he cried.

There was a little card below it. On it was written: TOOTHBRUSH FROM THE 1800S. IT MOST LIKELY BELONGED TO SOMEONE WHO LIVED IN SENECA VILLAGE. IT WAS FOUND FIVE YEARS AGO NEAR BELVEDERE CASTLE, IN A HOLE FILLED WITH WALNUTS.

9
Birthday Feast

"Hurry up, Cordelia!" Shakespeare called up to her tree house.

"Almost done!" Cordelia called back down. She tied a green ribbon around the present, then scrambled down the tree to where Shakespeare and Isaac were waiting.

Shakespeare had combed his tail and polished his whiskers. Isaac was wearing a dress shirt and a bow tie. Cordelia wore the most glittery thing she owned, which was her Wonder Woman costume.

"How come you're not wearing George the lobster hat?" Isaac asked.

"He did a lot of worrying today," Cordelia said. "He needed a rest."

"Wait for me! I'm coming, I'm coming!" Fenton was running toward them, the plastic beads on his tail clattering against the ground. When he reached them, he said, "What do you think? Am I fancy enough for the prince's birthday banquet?"

"I understood that!" Isaac cried. He had been working out the translation in his head. "He wants to know if he's fancy enough, right?"

"Right," said Cordelia.

Isaac took off his bow tie and tied it around Fenton's neck. "Now you're perfect!"

Belvedere Castle was filled with squirrels from all over the park. The halls were decorated with pine cones strung along the walls and tinfoil birds hanging from the ceiling.

All the squirrels in the neighborhood were there, including Kate and her sister, Bianca. Bianca was thrilled to see Cordelia, but Kate just sneered. "What are you doing here, Popsicle Stick Legs? This is a 'squirrels only' event. No people invited."

"Well, *some* people were invited," Cordelia said, "because super guess what? Here I am!"

Set out on a huge tree stump was a

delicious birthday feast of roasted chestnuts and baked acorns and pickled tree buds and a three-tiered hazelnut birthday cake with wild blueberry frosting.

When Fenton saw all that scrumptious food, he forgot he was supposed to be a fancy rat. He jumped onto the tree stump; then he climbed to the top of the birthday cake and took a big bite. The squirrels all gasped. Fenton stopped eating and looked around at their horrified faces.

Uh-oh.

But then Prince Oliver cried, "CAKE TIME!" before scrambling to the top of the cake and diving straight into it.

Prince Cedric climbed up next and yelled "Cannonball!" before he dove in after his brother. All the squirrel guests dove into the cake too (Cordelia and Isaac managed to plunge their hands into the cake and each pull out a fistful), until all that was left was a pile of crumbs.

After everyone had eaten the rest of the food, the

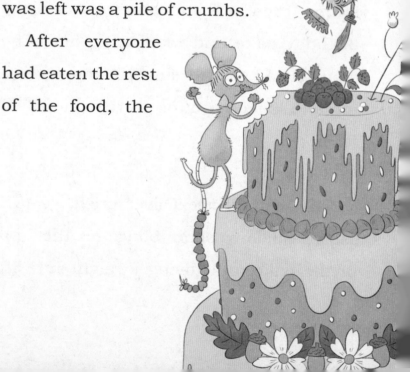

queen stood up and said, "Happy birthday to my youngest son Prince Oliver. Thanks to him, and to our dear friend Cordelia, the mystery of the Royal Scepter has been solved. King Alonso must have dropped the scepter accidentally when he was burying walnuts. He was always losing things. He lost his crown at least three times a day."

Cordelia smiled at Prince Oliver, who smiled back at her.

"Though we may not get the scepter back," the queen continued, "Cordelia has offered to take us to the museum to see it whenever we like."

The queen went up to Cordelia and

handed her a take-out container with MARTY'S ONION RINGS printed on the lid. "Cordelia, I present to you a special medal for your service. You are now an Honorary Squirrel of Central Park!"

Everyone clapped and cheered. Well, everyone except Kate, who looked very grumpy. Cordelia opened the take-out container. There were no onion rings inside. Instead, she found a necklace made of seeds with a silver medallion hanging from it. The medallion was actually the foil top of a pudding cup, but Cordelia thought it was the most beautiful necklace she'd ever seen.

After the feast Cordelia handed Prince Oliver his birthday present. "It's not a shark," she said before he could ask.

Prince Oliver unwrapped the gift, and when he saw what it was, he squeaked and jumped straight up. His crown flew off, but Cordelia caught it in midair and put it back on his head.

"What is it? What is it?" the other squirrels asked.

Prince Oliver held it up for everyone to see. It was white and smooshy and shaped like a large bowl.

"It's a diaper nest!" the prince cried.

"I was thinking," Cordelia said to Shakespeare, as she was getting into bed that night, "maybe some other girl from Seneca Village used to climb this very same elm tree years and years ago."

"I wouldn't be surprised," Shakespeare said. "It's a very old tree."

"Where do you think all those people from Seneca Village went? After they were forced to leave?"

"I'm not sure," Shakespeare replied. "Probably out there somewhere. In the city."

Even from the cozy shelter of the elm tree, they could hear the honking of horns and the wailing of sirens and the *fwhoosh* of car tires outside the park's walls.

"I bet they hated it," Cordelia said, "because it wasn't their home."

Shakespeare told her a story and tucked her into bed. But Cordelia lay awake for a long while afterward. As she snuggled under the covers, the sounds of the city felt far away. She might not be a squirrel, not a real one anyway, but she *did* belong here. She belonged here because it was her home. She belonged here because the squirrels counted on her, and she counted on them. She belonged here because there was no other place in the whole wide world that she would rather be than under the stars, in her elm tree, with Shakespeare in the park.

Acknowledgments

I am always and forever grateful to all the people who helped create this series. Huge thanks to my editor Karen Wojtyla, who is so clever that I bet she could learn Chittering in no time! Thanks to Nicole Fiorica and the whole Squirlish Squad at Margaret K. McElderry Books for their warmth and guidance. Big thanks to my extraordinary agent, Alice Tasman, who always has my back. Thanks to illustrator Sara Cristofori for bringing Cordelia and all the Central Park squirrels to life in the most charming way. Finally, thanks to Adam and Ian, my precious touchstones.

Cordelia is a girl raised by the squirrels of Central Park. Now she is on a journey to be—not exactly a girl, but more than a squirrel—squirlish!

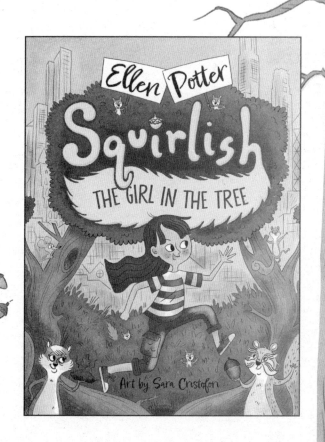

PRINT AND EBOOK EDITIONS AVAILABLE

Margaret K. McElderry Books • simonandschuster.com/kids